*Special thanks to twins
Rebekah MeiRui and Jennifer MeiDe Reed Kahn
Mae Lan and Sylvie Ling Pryor
Catherine and Margaret Gorman
Alexandra and Charlotte Zieselman
Kendal and Chelsea Tinsley
Mayalin and Kiralee Murphy
Janie and Suzie Romano*

Ling & Ting: Not Exactly the Same! copyright © 2010 by Grace Lin • Ling & Ting: Twice as Silly copyright © 2014 by Grace Lin • Ling & Ting: Together in All Weather copyright © 2015 by Grace Lin • Cover illustration copyright © 2010, 2024 by Grace Lin • Cover design by Saho Fujii and Patrick Collins • Cover copyright © 2024 by Hachette Book Group, Inc. • Hachette Book Group supports the right to free expression and the value of copyright. • The purpose of copyright is to encourage writers and artists to produce the creative works that enrich our culture. • The scanning, uploading, and distribution of this book without permission is a theft of the author's intellectual property. If you would like permission to use material from the book (other than for review purposes), please contact permissions@hbgusa.com. Thank you for your support of the author's rights. • Little, Brown and Company • Hachette Book Group • 1290 Avenue of the Americas, New York, NY 10104 • Visit us at LBYR.com • Ling & Ting: Not Exactly the Same! originally published by Little, Brown and Company in July 2010 • Ling & Ting: Twice as Silly originally published by Little, Brown and Company in November 2014 • Ling & Ting: Together in All Weather originally published by Little, Brown and Company in November 2015 • First Bind-Up Edition: May 2024 • Little, Brown and Company is a division of Hachette Book Group, Inc. • The Little, Brown name and logo are registered trademarks of Hachette Book Group, Inc. • The publisher is not responsible for websites (or their content) that are not owned by the publisher. • Little, Brown and Company books may be purchased in bulk for business, educational, or promotional use. For information, please contact your local bookseller or the Hachette Book Group Special Markets Department at special.markets@hbgusa.com. • Library of Congress Control Number: 2023949795 • ISBNs: 978-0-316-57792-2 (hardcover), 978-0-316-57793-9 (pbk.), 978-0-316-57794-6 (ebook) • PRINTED IN CHINA • APS

Hardcover: 10 9 8 7 6 5 4 3 2 1
Paperback: 10 9 8 7 6 5 4 3 2 1

Passport to Reading titles are leveled by independent reviewers applying the standards developed by Irene Fountas and Gay Su Pinnell in *Matching Books to Readers: Using Leveled Books in Guided Reading*, Heinemann, 1999.

Table of Contents

1. The Haircuts
2. The Magic Trick
3. Making Dumplings
4. Chopsticks
5. The Library Book
6. Mixed Up

Ling and Ting are twins. They have the same brown eyes. They have the same pink cheeks. They have the same happy smiles. People see them and they say, "You two are exactly the same!"

"We are not *exactly* the same," Ling says.

Ting laughs because she is thinking exactly the same thing!

Ling and Ting also have the same black hair. It grows long at the same time too. They are going to the barber for a haircut.

"You two are exactly the same!" the barber says.

"We are not *exactly* the same," Ting says.

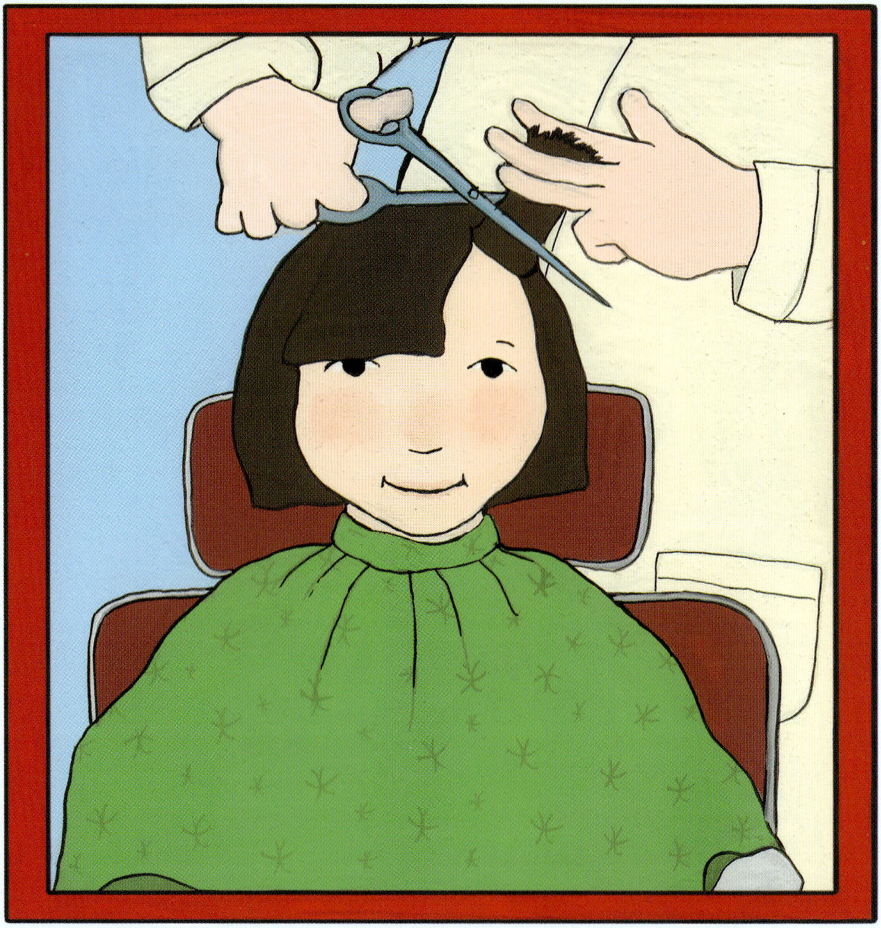

Ling sits in the chair. She does not move. Ling can always sit still. *Snip! Clip!* The barber cuts Ling's hair in a smooth line.

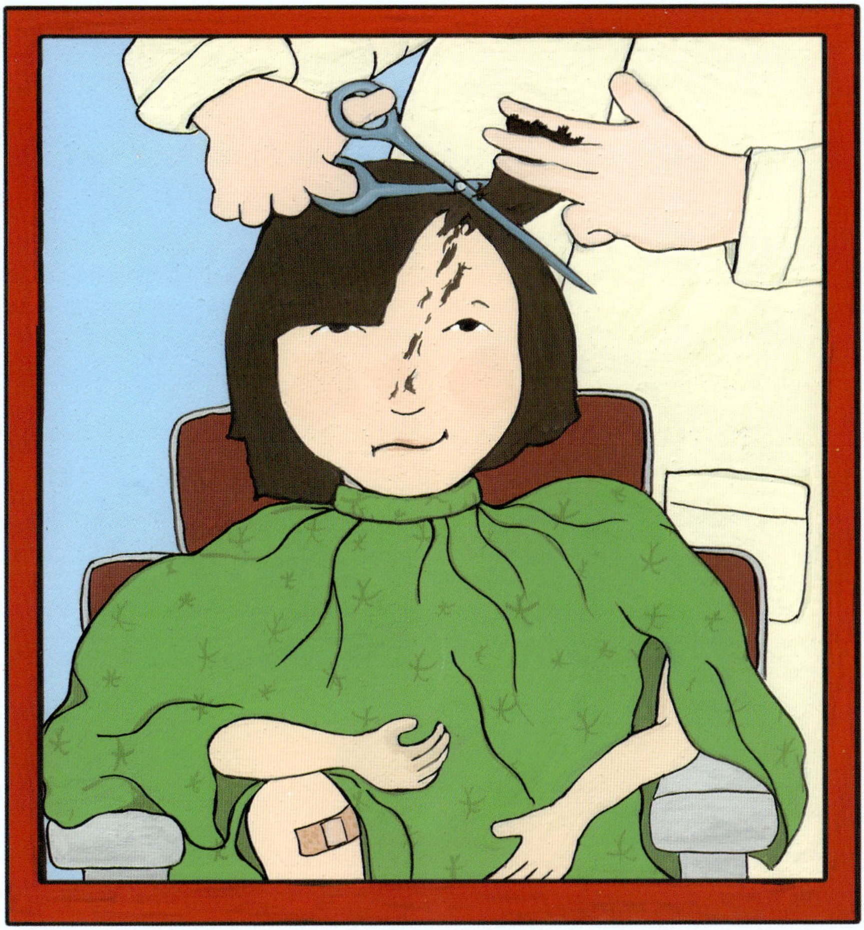

Now it is Ting's turn. She moves her legs and her fingers. Ting can never sit still. ***Snip! Clip!*** The barber cuts Ting's hair. It falls on her nose . . .

AHH-CHOOO!
Oh no!

Oops.

Ling and Ting are twins. They are not exactly the same. Now when people see them, they know it too.

Ling is wearing a big black hat. It is a very big hat. It is too big for Ling.

"Why are you wearing that hat?" Ting asks.

"It is a magic hat," Ling says. "I am wearing it because I can do magic."

"You can?" Ting says. "Can you use your magic to get a smaller hat?"

"No," Ling says. "But I can do a magic card trick."

Ling makes a pile of cards.

"Pick a card, any card," Ling says.

Ting picks a card.

"Now," Ling says, "put it back and mix the cards up."

Ting puts the card back and mixes the cards up.

"**Shazaam!**" Ling says and she waves her wand.

"Abracadabra! Hocus pocus!"

"Is this your card?" Ling asks.

"No," Ting says.

"Is this your card?" Ling asks.

"No," Ting says.

"This one?" asks Ling. "This one?"

"No," says Ting. "No."

"I give up," Ling says. "What is your card?"

Ting turns pink.

"I don't know," she says. "I forgot!"

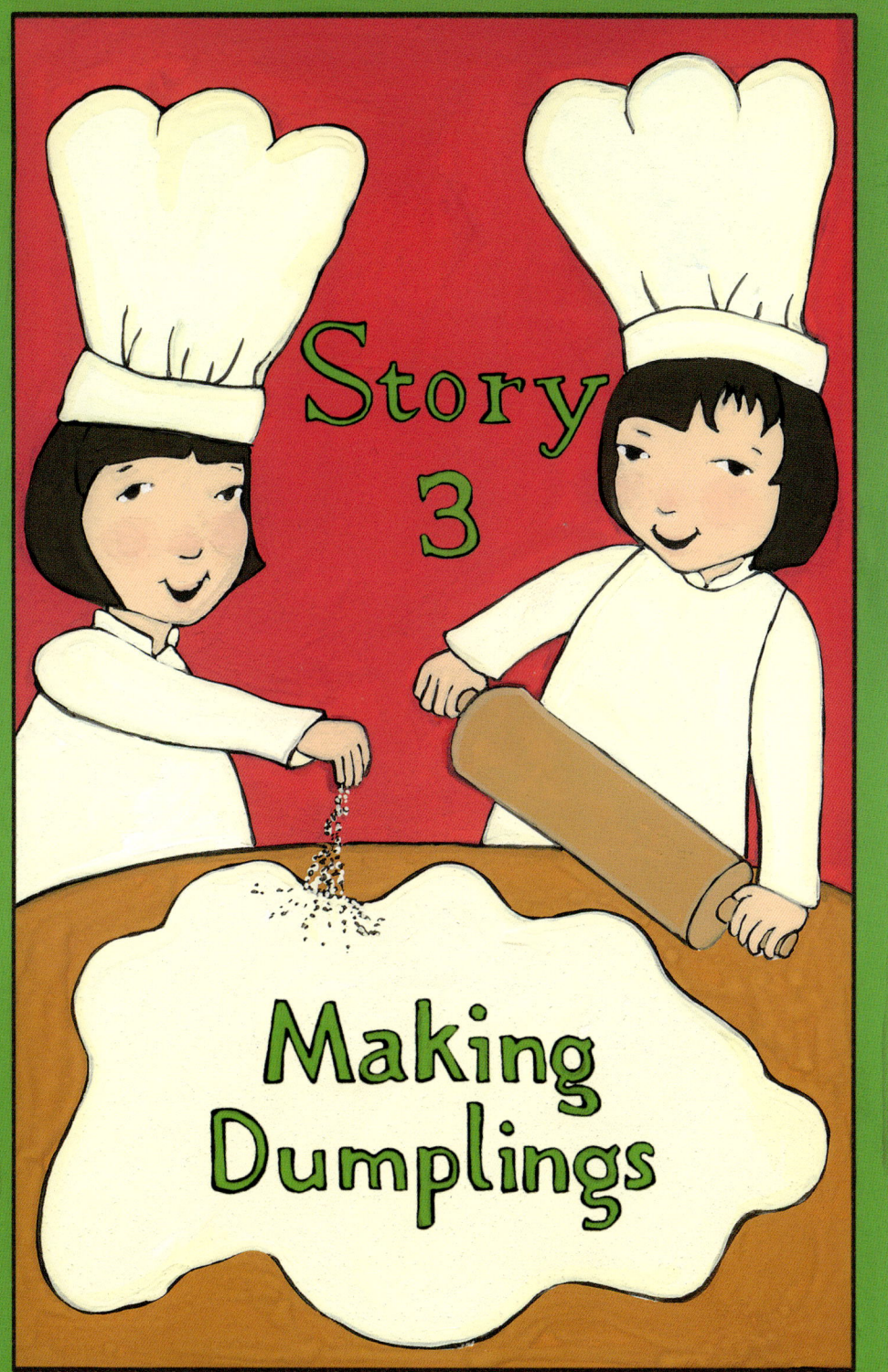

Ling and Ting are going to make dumplings.

"People say dumplings look like old Chinese money," Ling says.

"We should make a lot of dumplings," Ting says. "Then we will have a lot of money."

So, Ling rolls and Ting mixes.

"I will close my dumplings tight," Ling says. "Then our money will not get away."

"I will put a lot of meat in my dumplings," Ting says. "So we will be very rich."

Soon all the dumplings are done.

"Our dumplings do not look the same," Ling says. "My dumplings are smooth. Your dumplings are fat."

"Yours are dump-Lings," Ting says. "Mine are dump-*Tings!*"

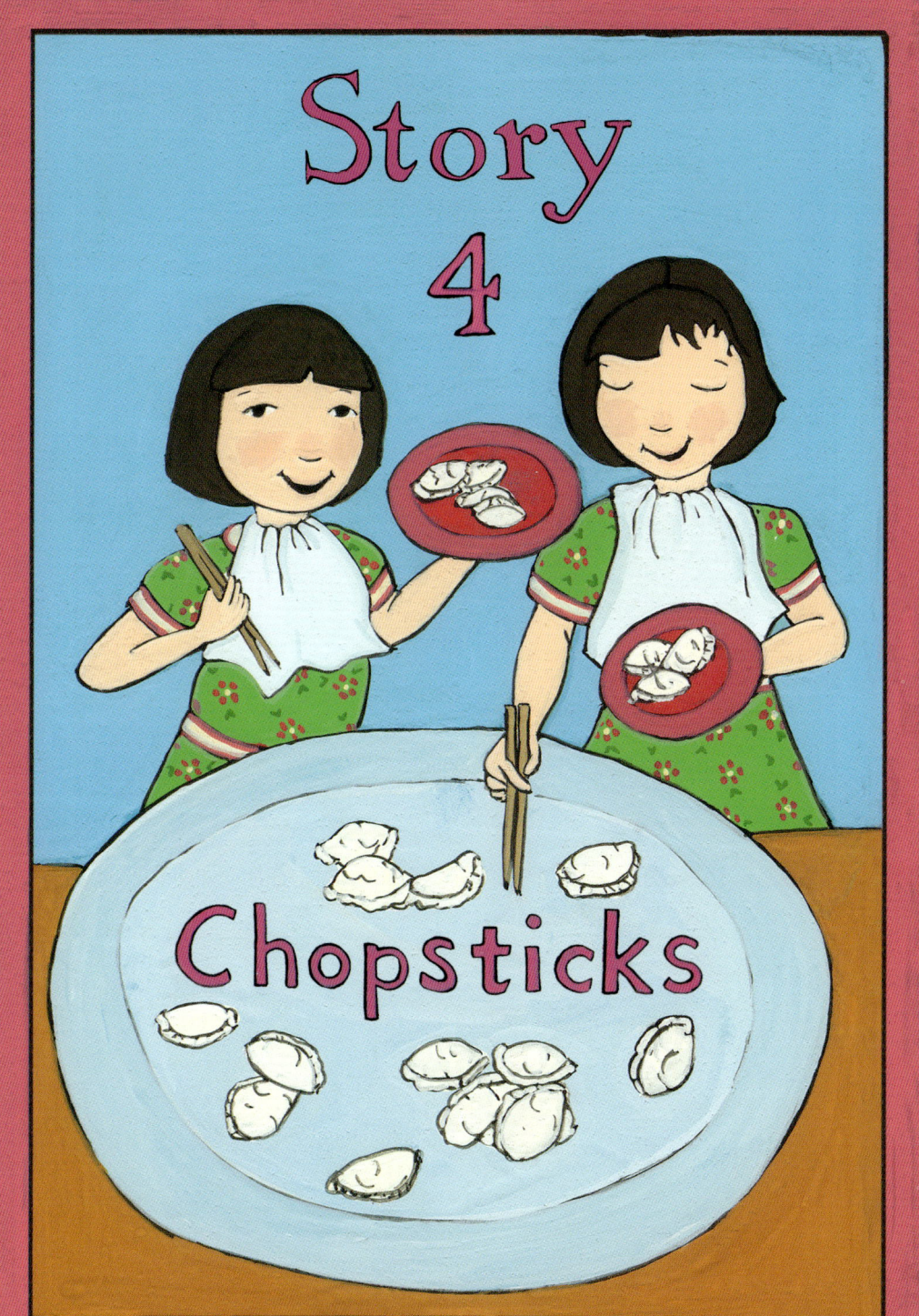

At dinner, Ling cannot eat.

"Chopsticks are tricky," Ling says. "They are hard to use."

"Chopsticks are not tricky," Ting says. "They are not hard to use."

"Chopsticks are hard for *me* to use," Ling says. "I cannot eat. My food falls off my chopsticks."

"I know!" Ting says. "We can glue the food to your chopsticks."

"Glue!" Ling says. "That would make the food taste bad!"

"I know!" Ting says. "We can tie the food to your chopsticks."

"Tie?" Ling asks. "That would be messy."

"I know!" Ting says. "I will feed you with *my* chopsticks."

"No!" Ling says. "I do not want to glue my chopsticks. I do not want to tie my chopsticks. I do not want you to feed me with your chopsticks."

"Then how will you eat?" Ting asks.

"I will eat with a fork," Ling says.

Story 5

The Library Book

"I am going to the library," Ting says. "I am going to get a fairy tale book."

"Will you get me a book?" Ling asks. "Get me a book about dogs."

At the library, Ting looks at all the books. Then, Ting sees a book with fairy tales.

"I must see Ling right away!" Ting says. She runs back home.

"Ling! Ling!" Ting says. "I remember my card! It was the King of Hearts!"

"That is good," Ling says. "Did you get me a book about dogs?"

Ting turns pink.

"Oops," she says, "I forgot!"

"Tell me a story," Ling says.

"Okay," Ting says. "Once upon a time, there were twin girls. They were named Ling and Ting. People saw them and said, 'You two are exactly the same!'"

"Oh good," Ling says. "I know this story."

"Then, one day, Ling sneezed during her haircut. . . . ," Ting says.

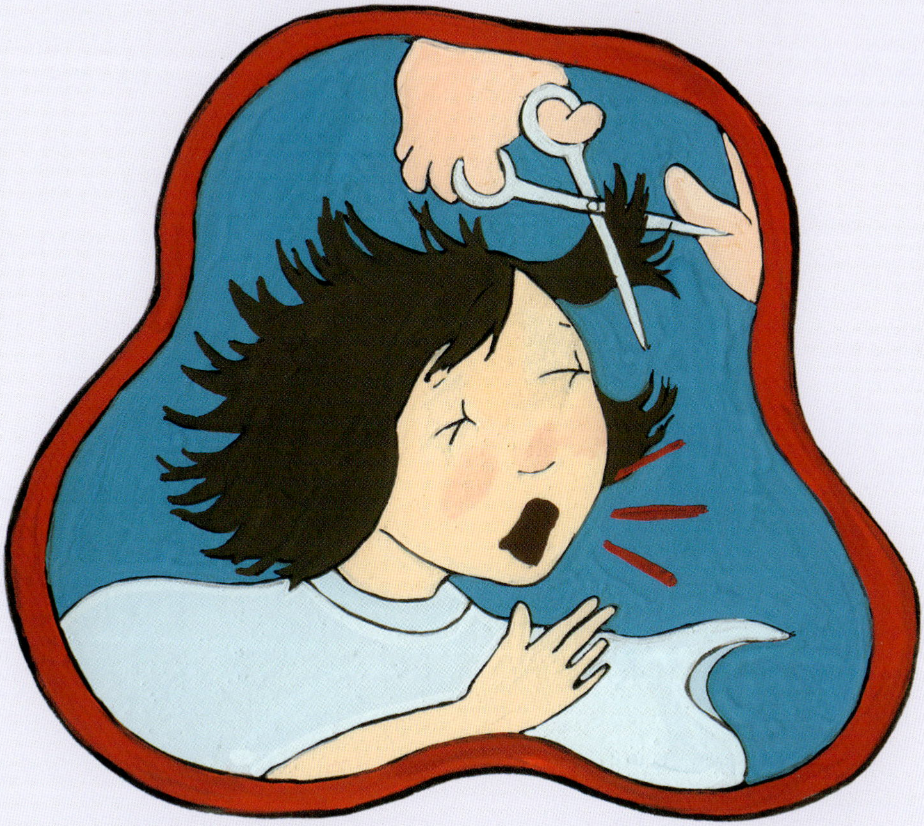

"You mixed that up," Ling says. "You sneezed, not me!"

"When Ling sneezed, her magic hat flew . . . ," Ting says.

"My magic hat flew?" asks Ling.

"It flew to Ting. She put it on and waved her chopstick. She turned the dumplings into money . . ."

"Chopstick? Dumplings?" asks Ling.

" . . . for the King of Hearts. He couldn't decide if he wanted to marry Ling or Ting. . . . "

"Marry?" says Ling. "What?!"

"Oh, Ting," Ling says, "you mixed up the whole story!"

"But the twins told the king to go away. They were not exactly the same," Ting says, "but they always stayed together."

"Well," Ling says, "at least you got the ending right."

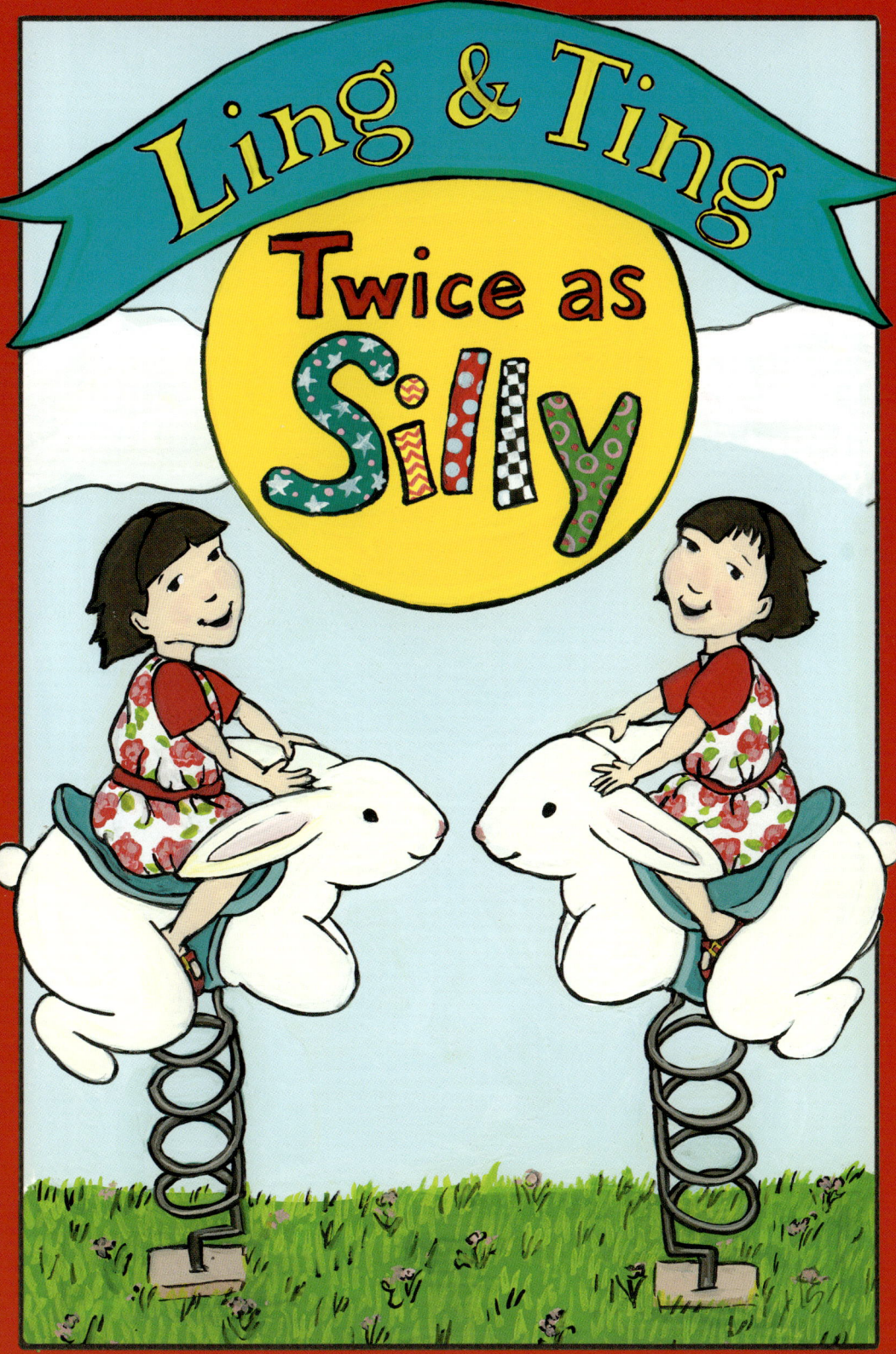

Double thanks to twins Emily and Olivia

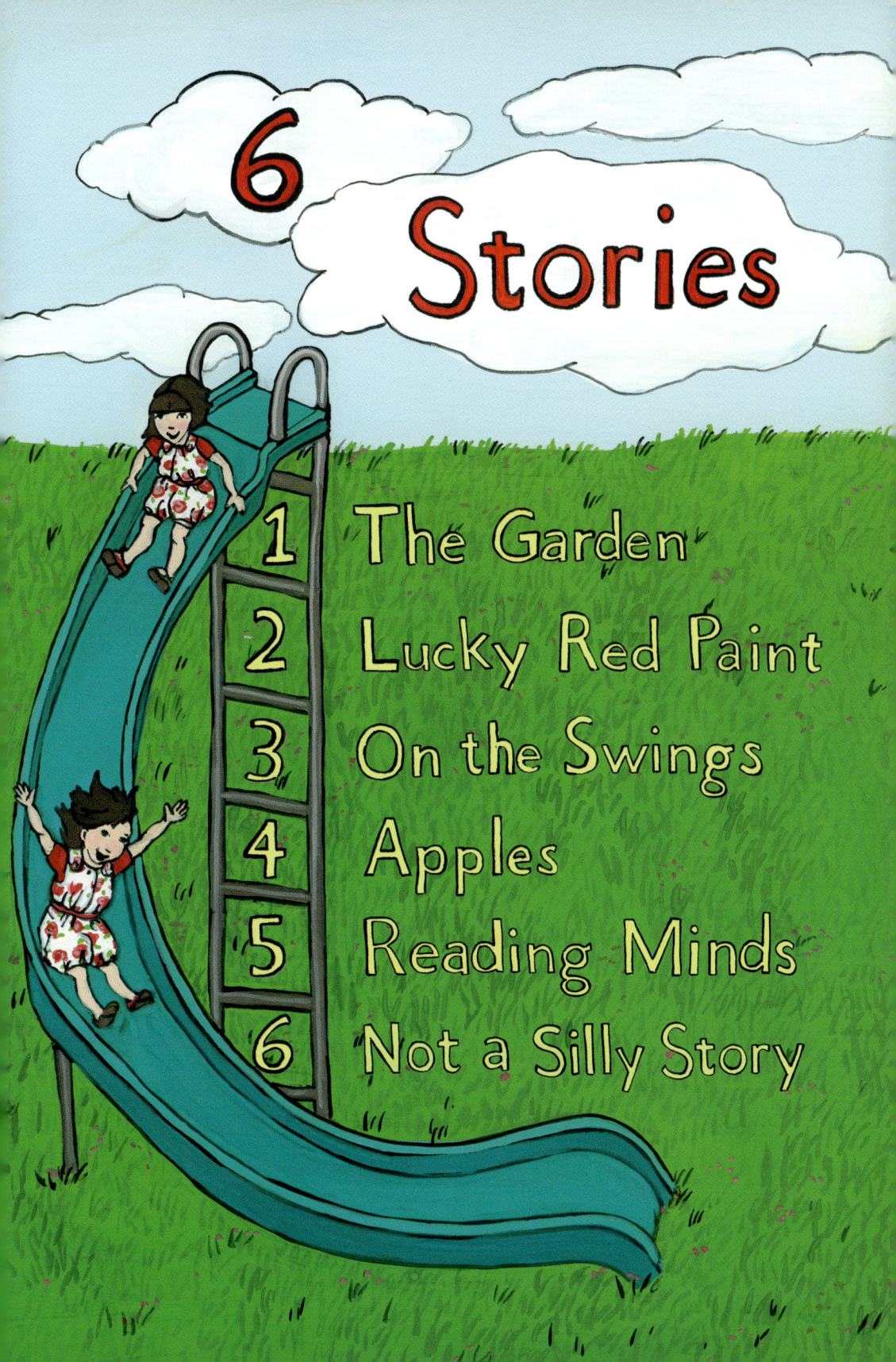

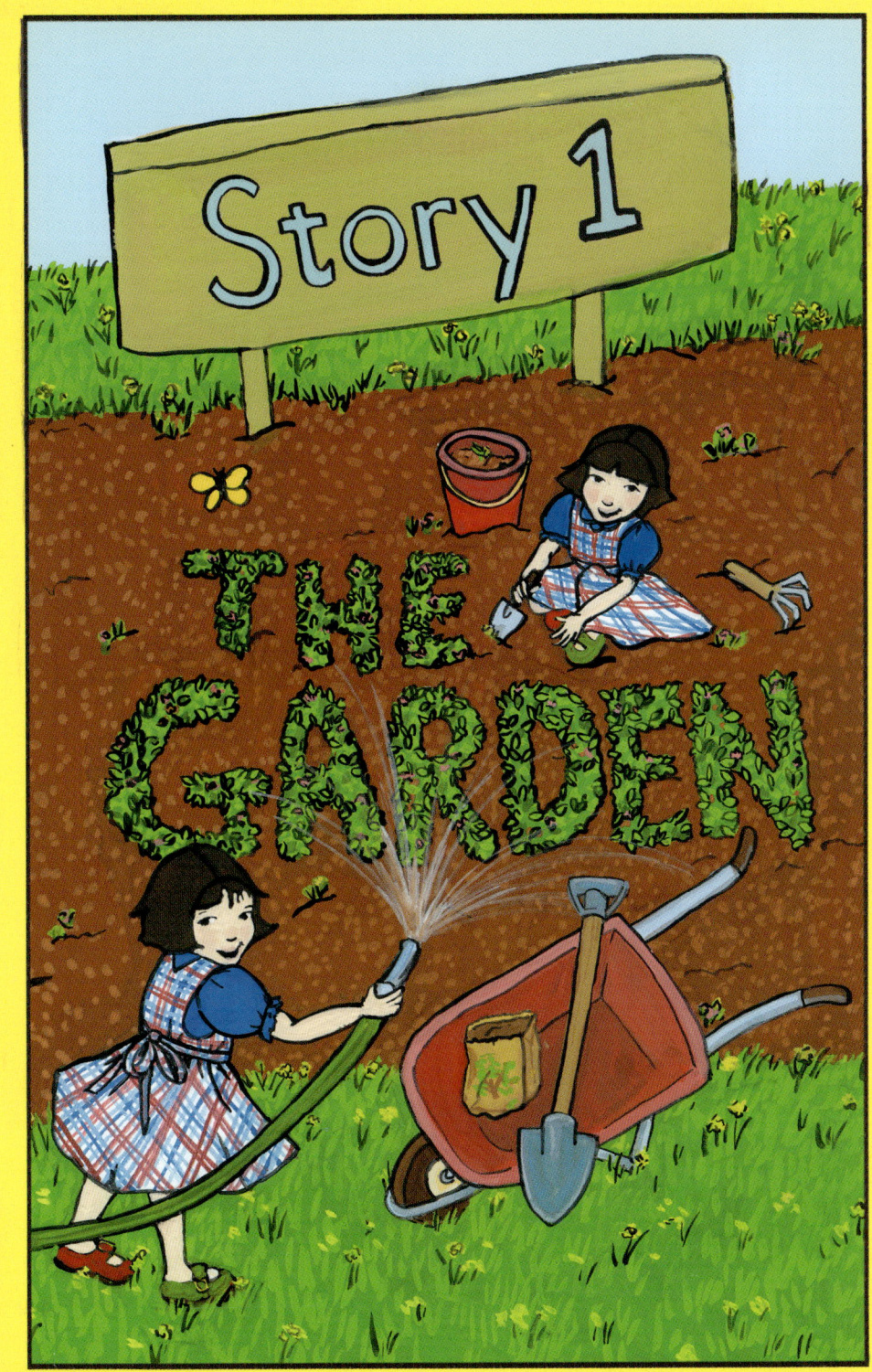

Ting is in the garden.

"What are you doing?" Ling asks.

"I am planting cupcakes," Ting says.

"Ting!" Ling says. "You cannot plant cupcakes."

Ting digs a hole. She puts in a cupcake. She covers the hole.

"See!" Ting says.
"I can plant cupcakes."

"Ting!" Ling says. "Cupcakes will not grow. Cupcakes are not seeds. Seeds grow."

"I will try anyway," Ting says.

Day after day, Ting weeds and waters her garden.

Ting waits, but nothing grows.

"Ling," Ting says, "you are right. I will not have a cupcake garden. Cupcakes will not grow."

"Cupcakes are not seeds," Ling says. "Seeds grow."

"Are beans seeds?" Ting asks.

"Yes," Ling says. "Beans are seeds."

"Good," Ting says. "Then next I will plant jelly beans."

Story 2
Lucky Red Paint

Ling is at the table. She has a paintbrush and a can of red paint.

"What are you doing?" Ting asks.

"I am painting my toys red," Ling says. "Red is a lucky Chinese color. I want my toys to be lucky. Do you want to paint?"

"Yes," Ting says. "I want to paint."

"You can paint now," Ling says. "I will get more paint."

"What should I paint?" Ting says.

"Paint everything," Ling says. "I will be back soon."

Ting likes to paint. She likes to paint fast. When Ting paints, the paint splashes. It splashes on Ting.

When Ling comes back, Ting is covered with paint. Ling laughs hard.

"Ting!" Ling says. "I said 'Paint everything'! I did not say 'Paint everyTING'!"

Ling and Ting are at the playground. They are playing on the swings.

"How high can you swing?" Ting asks Ling.

"I can swing higher than a tree," Ling says.

"You can?" Ting asks. "Which tree?"

"Any tree," Ling says.

"Any tree?" Ting asks. "A tree that is taller than a giraffe?"

"Yes," Ling says.

"A tree that is taller than a building?" Ting asks.

"Yes," Ling says.

"A tree that is taller than a mountain?" Ting asks.

"Yes," Ling says.

"A tree that is higher than the clouds?" Ting asks.

"Yes," Ling says.

"A tree that goes into outer space?" Ting says. "A tree that is higher than the moon? A tree that is as high as the stars?"

"Yes," Ling says. "Yes. Yes."

"Okay," Ting says. "Show me how you can swing higher than a tree."

"I am doing it right now," Ling says. "We both are."

"We are?" Ting asks. "How?"

"It is easy to swing higher than a tree," Ling says. "A tree cannot swing."

"Look up there," Ting says. "There are apples. I want to eat them. Let us pick them."

"The apples are too high," Ling says. "We cannot climb that high."

"A monkey can climb that high," Ting says. "Let us get a monkey! A monkey will get us an apple."

"A monkey?" Ling asks. "How will we get a monkey?"

"We will go to the zoo," says Ting. "We will take a monkey from a cage."

"The cage will be locked at the zoo," says Ling. "Only the zookeeper has a key."

"A penguin will sneak the key for us," Ting says. "We will train a penguin to get the key."

"A penguin?" Ling asks. "How will we train a penguin?"

"We will feed the penguin a fish," Ting says. "Penguins will do anything for fish."

"We do not have any fish," Ling says. "How will we get a fish?"

"We will catch one," Ting says. "All we need is a worm."

"Where will we get a worm?" Ling says.

"We can get a worm in an apple," Ting says.

"Ting!" Ling says. "It is an apple we want! We do not want an apple for a worm! We want an apple to eat!"

"But how will we get one?" Ting says.

Ling climbs down.

"Come with me!" Ling says. "I know how we will get apples."

Ling brings Ting to the store. They buy many apples.

Ling and Ting are reading books together.

"Ting," Ling says, "this book says some twins are special."

"Are we special?" Ting asks.

"Special twins can read minds," Ling says.

"Oh," Ting says. "Let us see if we are special."

"Okay," Ling says. "I will think of something. What am I thinking of?"

Ling looks at Ting. Ting looks at Ling. Ting scratches her head.

"It is something spelled with four letters," Ling says. "It begins with *b*."

Ling holds her book. Ting looks at the book.

"Are you thinking of a book?" Ting asks.

"Yes!" Ling says. "You did it! You read my mind! Now I will read your mind."

Ling looks at Ting. Ting looks at Ling. Ling shakes her head.

"Nothing," Ling says. "My mind is reading nothing."

"Ling! You are right!" Ting says. "I was thinking nothing!"

Story 6

Not a Silly Story

"Let us write a story," Ting says.

"Yes," Ling says. "But we will not write a silly story."

"Okay," Ting says. "It will not be silly."

Ling begins, "Ling and Ting were two girls. . . ."

"Let us not be girls," Ting says. "Let us be rabbits!"

"Okay," Ling says. "Ling and Ting were two rabbits. One day they found an apple tree. . . ."

> They found ~~an apple~~ a cupcake tree. The cupcakes were at the top of the tree.

"Not an apple tree," says Ting. "Let us make it a cupcake tree."

"Okay," Ling says. "One day they found a cupcake tree. They could not reach the cupcakes. They had to use a lucky red toy to jump."

"Yes," Ting says. "They jumped higher than the tree. They jumped into outer space!"

"Outer space?" Ling says.

"Yes!" Ting says. "Then Rabbit Ling said to Rabbit Ting, 'How will we get down?'"

"But you cannot talk in outer space," Ling says. "Outer space has no sound."

"Ling and Ting were special rabbits," Ting says. "They could read minds! So, with her mind, Ting told Ling to eat stars!"

"How could they eat stars?" asks Ling.

"The stars were really jelly beans," Ting says. "After Ling and Ting ate them, they were very heavy. They sank down to Earth."

After eating the jelly bean stars, Ling and Ting were very heavy. They sank back down to Earth.

> On their way down, they picked some cupcakes. They ate the cupcakes for dessert.
> **THE END**

"What about the cupcake tree?" Ling says.

"They picked some cupcakes on their way down," Ting says. "That night, they had cupcakes for dessert after dinner. The end."

"Ting," Ling says, "I said we would not write a silly story."

"This is not a silly story," Ting says. "This is a very, very silly story!"

"You are right," Ling says. "It is very, very silly."

"Just like us," Ting says.

"Yes," Ling says. "Just like us."

Ling & Ting

Together in All Weather

To Alex,
who has been with me
through all weather

Ling and Ting are twins. They live together. They eat together. They play together. They are always together.

They are together when the wind blows. Outside, the sky is dark. The trees sway. The rain falls. There is thunder and lightning.

Lightning flashes. *Crack!*

"Eek!" says Ling.

"Are you scared of the storm?" Ting asks.

"No!" says Ling. "I am not scared! I was just surprised."

Boom! The thunder is loud.

"Eek!" says Ting.

"Are you scared of the storm?" Ling asks.

"No!" Ting says. "I am not scared. I was just surprised, too."

Lightning flashes. *Crack!*

Boom! The thunder is loud.

"Eek!" Ling and Ting say together.

They sit close to each other. They put a blanket over their heads.

"We are not scared," Ling says.

"No," Ting says. "We are just surprised."

Ling and Ting are twins. They are always together. They are surprised together, too.

The sun is bright. It is hot.

"Ting," Ling says, "I have an idea. Let us make lemonade. We will sell it. We will make a lot of money."

"Yes!" Ting says. "Let us sell lemonade!"

Ling cuts the lemons. Ting adds the water, sugar, and ice. They take the lemonade outside. They take a little box for money outside, too.

The sun is bright. It is hot. No one comes to buy the lemonade. Ling and Ting wait.

"I would like some lemonade," Ting says.

"Ting," Ling says, "the lemonade is for sale. You must buy the lemonade."

Ting buys a glass of lemonade. She gives Ling a nickel. Ling puts it in the little box.

"Now we have earned a nickel," Ling says.

"Hmmm," Ting says.

"I would like some lemonade," Ling says.

"You must buy it, too," Ting says.

Ling buys a glass of lemonade. She gives Ting a nickel.

Ting puts it in the little box with the other nickel.

"Now we have earned two nickels," Ting says.

"Hmmm," Ling says.

"Ling," Ting says, "there are two nickels in the box. We have earned two nickels together."

"Yes," Ling says. "There is one nickel for you and one nickel for me."

"I will take my nickel now," says Ting. She takes one nickel from the box.

"I would like to buy another glass of lemonade," says Ting. She gives Ling the nickel. Ling puts the nickel back into the box.

Then Ting drinks another glass of lemonade. Ling watches her.

"I will take my nickel now, too," says Ling. She takes a nickel from the box. Then she gives the nickel to Ting. "I would like to buy another glass of lemonade, too."

The sun is bright. It is hot. Ling and Ting buy more lemonade. Ling and Ting drink more lemonade. Soon the lemonade is gone.

"Good job!" Ting says. "We sold all the lemonade!"

"Yes," Ling says. "We did sell all the lemonade. But we did not make a lot of money."

It is cool outside. The leaves are yellow, red, and orange. They are falling from the trees. Ling and Ting are raking leaves.

"Raking is hard work," Ting says. She feels hot. She takes off her hat.

Soon all the leaves are in a big pile.

"We are finished!" Ling says.

Ting nods. Then Ting scratches her head.

"Where is my hat?" Ting asks.

Ting looks for her red hat. Ling helps her. They look through the big pile of leaves. Soon there is no pile. They cannot find the hat.

Then Ling looks at the tree. "Look at that funny red leaf!" says Ling. "It looks like—"

"My hat!" says Ting. "We found my hat!"

Ting is happy. But Ling is not happy. Ling looks at the leaves. There are leaves everywhere. There is no pile of leaves.

"Oops," Ting says. "We must rake again."

Ling nods. Then Ling scratches her head.

"Where is my hat?" Ling asks.

"It is winter," says Ling. "Now we must shovel snow. Ting, let us go shovel the snow."

Ting does not want to shovel the snow. Ting thinks hard. She gets into her bed. She rubs her nose.

"I am sick," Ting says. "I cannot go outside. I cannot shovel the snow."

"You are sick?" Ling asks. "If you are sick, you need medicine. I will make you some."

"You will make me medicine?" Ting asks.

"Yes," Ling says. "I have a recipe. It is for an old Chinese medicine. It works well."

In the kitchen, Ling makes the medicine. She cooks onions, ginger, and water. She adds mustard and garlic. She adds sticks and dirt. She adds a sock and a shoelace. Ting watches from the door.

"Almost done!" Ling says. She stirs the medicine. The medicine looks bad. The medicine smells bad.

"Ling!" Ting says. "I think I am better now. I am not sick. I do not need old Chinese medicine."

"Are you sure?" Ling asks.

"Yes," Ting says. "It is winter. We must shovel snow."

"Good," says Ling. "The old Chinese medicine really does work well."

The snow is melting. The air is warm. Spring is coming.

"Soon it will be spring," Ling says. "Soon there will be leaves. Soon there will be flowers!"

"Look!" Ting says. "There is already a flower!"

"It is the first flower of spring!" Ling says. "Let us go see it!"

Ling and Ting go to the flower. They look at it. Ting scratches her head.

"It is a funny flower!" Ting says. "It looks like—"

"My hat!" Ling says. "We found my hat!"

"Ling! Look at the strange weather," Ting says. "There is sun and there is rain. There are both at the same time."

"Ting," Ling says, "this is rainbow weather! This is when we can find a rainbow!"

"It is?" Ting asks. "Let us go look for a rainbow! If we find one, we will be lucky!"

Ling looks behind the house. She does not see a rainbow.

Ting looks in front of the house. She does not see a rainbow.

"I looked behind the house," Ling tells Ting. "I did not find a rainbow."

"I looked in front of the house," Ting tells Ling. "I did not find a rainbow, either."

"Let us go to the big hill," Ling says. "We will look for a rainbow together."

Ling and Ting walk up the big hill. The rain still falls. The sun still shines. When they reach the top of the hill, they look for a rainbow.